GEORGE
AND DIGGETY

by Maggie Stern

illustrations by
Blanche Sims

ORCHARD BOOKS • NEW YORK

Orchard Books, A Grolier Company
95 Madison Avenue, New York, NY 10016

Manufactured in the United States of America
Printed and bound by Phoenix Color Corp.
Book design by Helene Berinsky
The text of this book is set in 18 point Goudy.
The illustrations are pen and ink with watercolor.

Hardcover 10 9 8 7 6 5 4 3 2 1
Paperback 10 9 8 7 6 5 4 3 2 1

Library of Congress Cataloging-in-Publication Data
Stern, Maggie.
George and Diggety / by Maggie Stern; illustrations by Blanche Sims.
p. cm.
Summary: George tests his dog's IQ, takes him sledding, and gives Diggety
a birthday dinner with homemade dog biscuits. Includes recipe.
ISBN 0-531-30295-4 (trade : alk. paper)
ISBN 0-531-33295-0 (lib. bdg. : alk. paper)
ISBN 0-531-07172-3 (pbk. : alk. paper)
[1. Dogs—Fiction.] I. Sims, Blanche, ill. II. Title.
PZ7.S83875 Gj 2000
[Fic]—dc21   99-58612

Contents

Dog Test

George was reading his dog magazine.

Diggety sniffed the floor for crumbs.

"Are you still reading that?"

asked George's sister, Lulu.

"Listen," said George.

"Here is a test you can give your dog

to tell how smart he is."

"Cool," said their older brother, Henry.

"There are ten questions," said George.

"The dog gets points for
how well he does on each one.

He can score up to one hundred points.

We will find out if Diggety is a genius!"

George cleared his throat.

"Ready, Diggety?"

Diggety was licking up cracker crumbs.

"Let me keep score," said Lulu.

"Here are the directions," she said.

"You have to choose answer

A, B, or C for each question."

"O.K.," said George.

"The first question is:

'If you ask your dog

to fetch his ball, will he

A) get the ball and bring it to you?

B) get the ball and run off with it?

C) look at you as if you are crazy?'"

George pointed under the table.

"Diggety," he said,

"get me your ball!"

Diggety yawned.

"Come on, Diggety. Fetch!"

Diggety cocked his head.

"Watch me," George said.

George crawled under the

kitchen table.

He took the ball and

showed it to Diggety.

"See how easy it is," George said.

He put down the ball

and backed away.

"Now *you* do it!"

Diggety barked.

He sniffed for more crumbs.

Lulu wrote something down.

"My turn to ask a question," said Henry.

"'If you take a ball and pretend

to throw it across the room, will your dog

A) run after it?

B) start to run but see that you did not

throw it?

C) sit and wait for you to really throw it?'"

Henry squeezed the ball so Diggety

would hear the squeaky noise.

Diggety looked up.

Henry pretended to throw the ball

out the door.

"Go get it, Diggety," Henry called.

Diggety dashed into the dining room.

Henry tossed the ball from

hand to hand.

George brought Diggety back

from the dining room.

"Try that again," George said.

"Diggety, this time,

when Henry moves his arm,

watch what I do."

Henry pretended to throw

the ball again.

George watched Henry.

He did not move.

Diggety charged into

the dining room again.

Lulu rolled her eyes.

She marked her score pad.

"Third question," George said.

"'If your dog watches someone get hurt, will he

A) go find help?

B) stay beside the hurt person and
   lick his face?

C) run off and play?'"

"I will do this one," said Henry.

He flung himself on the floor.

Henry shouted.

He pretended his leg was hurt.

"Help me, Diggety! Go get help!"

Diggety wagged his tail.

He ran and picked up the ball.

"No, Diggety!" said George.

"Go get help! Do what I do."

George ran to Lulu.

He pulled her to Henry.

Diggety barked at the ball.

"This is hopeless," George said,

falling on the floor.

Diggety dropped the ball in George's lap.

After the last question,

George looked at Lulu.

"Tell me the score," he said.

Lulu counted the points.

She looked at George.

"Which do you want first," Lulu asked,

"the good news or the bad news?"

George scratched his head.

"The bad news, I guess."

"Diggety does not test well," said Lulu.

"He scored one point for effort."

George sighed.

"What is the good news?" he asked.

Lulu smiled.

"You scored one hundred points.

George, you are a genius!"

Sledding

"YIPPEE!" shouted George.

"It is snowing hard. No school!"

"Great," said Henry.

"A snow day."

"We can go sledding!" said George.

"We can go to the big hill."

George ran outside.

He opened his mouth

to catch the flakes.

Diggety rolled in the snow.

Lulu took out the sleds.

"I get the orange one,"

she said.

"I get the fast one,"

said George.

Diggety barked.

"I get the tube,"

said Henry.

George pulled his sled to the top

and soared down.

Diggety ran beside him, barking.

George got to the bottom of the hill first.

George hopped off his sled.

He dragged it back up

and slid down again.

"My sled is heavy," said George,

pulling it up the hill.

"Mine too," said Lulu.

"That is the worst part of sledding,"
said Henry.

"I have an idea," said George.

He took the sled rope and

put it in Diggety's mouth.

"See you at the top, Diggety."

Diggety charged up the hill.

George raced after him.

"You win," George said, out of breath.

Then George lay on the sled
and zoomed down.

"My turn," said Lulu.

She gave Diggety her sled rope.

Diggety wagged his tail
while running up the hill.
"Diggety is one strong dog,"
said Henry.
He gave Diggety the rope to his tube.
"Way to go," Henry said,
flying down the hill.

"My turn," said George.

This time, Diggety trudged up the hill.

The sled thumped behind him.

But even without the sled, George

was too tired to move.

The hill was big.

His toes were cold.

George watched Diggety reach

the top of the hill.

"Diggety, come get me,"

called George.

Diggety sat down next to the sled.

"Diggety, COME!" ordered George.

Diggety looked around.

Then he hopped on the sled.

The sled began to move.

Diggety was sledding down the hill!

He sailed past George.

When the sled stopped,

Diggety jumped off

and dragged it over to George.

"What a dog!" George exclaimed.

George took the sled rope.

"Hop back on, Diggety!" George said.

"It is my turn to give you a ride!"

Diggety's Birthday

"Can we have a birthday dinner
for Diggety?" asked George.
"Sounds like fun to me!" said Lulu.
"Who ever heard of a
birthday dinner for a dog?"
said Henry.

"I will plan the menu," said George.

"Hamburgers for us."

"And for Diggety?" asked Lulu.

"Hmm." George scratched his head.

"I know! We can make him dog biscuits."

"Now I have heard everything,"

said Henry.

"Next you will invite the dogs

on the block and give them goody bags."

At the pet store, the woman
at the counter held up a cookie cutter
in the shape of a dog bone.
"This comes in a box with
a biscuit recipe on the back,"
said the woman.
"Perfect," said George.

George mixed the ingredients in a bowl.

Then he rolled the dough

and put it in the refrigerator.

Diggety sat on the floor and watched.

George flattened the dough

and cut it with the cutters.

Mom put the biscuits in the oven.

Diggety sniffed.

George paced.

"How many more minutes?" he asked.

"Fifteen," said Mom.

She pointed to the refrigerator.

"Please take out the hamburger patties."

George put the meat outside

on the table.

After fifteen minutes,

Mom took the biscuits out of the oven.

Diggety wagged his tail.

He stood on his hind legs.

George picked up one

of the biscuits from the basket.

It was warm.

It smelled good.

George popped the dog biscuit

into his mouth.

It was gone in one bite.

"Yum," he said.

"They taste like cheese crackers!"

He reached for another.

"Let me try one," said Lulu.

"Heavenly!"

She sighed.

Diggety howled.

"Now me," said Dad. "Tasty! Reminds me of the cheese sticks Granny used to bake. Diggety, stop that begging!" scolded Dad.

"My turn," said Henry. He ate a biscuit. "Awesome." Henry grabbed a handful. "Diggety, stop begging! Go away," ordered Henry. The doorbell rang.

42

"I have a package for you,"
said the mailman.
He sniffed the air.
"Macaroni and cheese?"
he asked.
George handed him a biscuit.
"Dog biscuits?" the mailman said.
"You do not expect me
to eat dog biscuits!"
"Try one," said George, licking his lips.
The mailman ate it.

"Delicious. If I roll over,

can I have another?"

"Now a biscuit for Diggety," said George.

"OH, NO!" he shouted.

"There are none left!"

Everyone was silent.

"Where is Diggety, anyway?" said George.

"Diggety!" yelled George.

"Diggety!" called Mom and Dad.

George ran to the backyard.

"Here he is!" called George.

"I am sorry, Diggety!"

George kneeled down

and kissed him on the nose.

"We did not mean to eat

all of your biscuits!"

Diggety was wagging his tail.

Diggety was licking his lips.

"Why are you so happy?" asked George.

"I think I know," Mom said.

George looked at the table.

The plate was there

but not the hamburgers!

George stared at Diggety.

Diggety stared at George.

"It is okay, Diggety," George said.

He patted Diggety's head.

"You had your birthday dinner

after all."

George grinned.

"And we did too!"

47

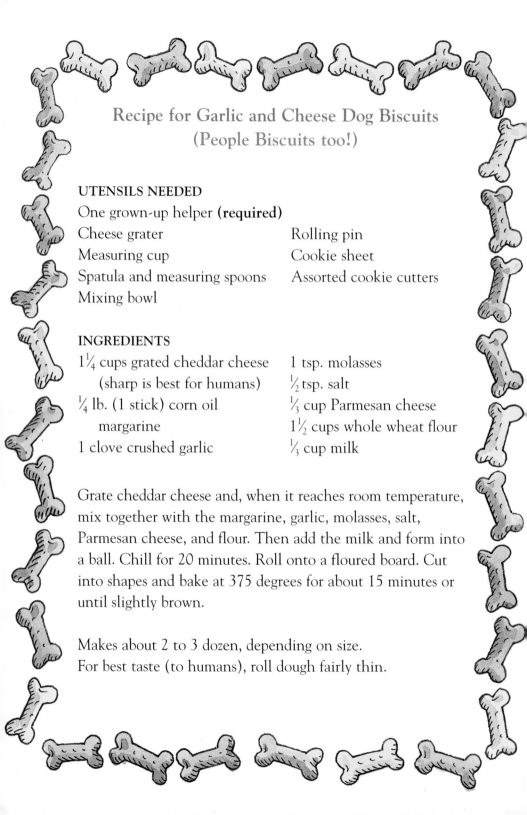

Recipe for Garlic and Cheese Dog Biscuits
(People Biscuits too!)

UTENSILS NEEDED

One grown-up helper **(required)**

Cheese grater

Measuring cup

Spatula and measuring spoons

Mixing bowl

Rolling pin

Cookie sheet

Assorted cookie cutters

INGREDIENTS

$1\frac{1}{4}$ cups grated cheddar cheese
  (sharp is best for humans)

$\frac{1}{4}$ lb. (1 stick) corn oil
  margarine

1 clove crushed garlic

1 tsp. molasses

$\frac{1}{2}$ tsp. salt

$\frac{1}{3}$ cup Parmesan cheese

$1\frac{1}{2}$ cups whole wheat flour

$\frac{1}{3}$ cup milk

Grate cheddar cheese and, when it reaches room temperature, mix together with the margarine, garlic, molasses, salt, Parmesan cheese, and flour. Then add the milk and form into a ball. Chill for 20 minutes. Roll onto a floured board. Cut into shapes and bake at 375 degrees for about 15 minutes or until slightly brown.

Makes about 2 to 3 dozen, depending on size.
For best taste (to humans), roll dough fairly thin.